All Aboard!

Contents	Page

written by Rachel Walker

Before trains were invented, people had to walk or use horses and wagons to get from place to place.

It was slow, tiring, and sometimes the weather made it difficult, so most people couldn't travel far from their homes. It wasn't unusual for people to never see the sea in their whole lifetime if they didn't live near the coast!

rocket locomotive

In the early 1800s the first locomotives were built in England. They ran on steam made by burning coal to heat water. As the water boiled, steam was produced to power the engines and drive the wheels.

By the 1830s, miles and miles of tracks were being laid all over the world, linking towns and cities. Rails were made of strong steel or iron that wouldn't buckle in the sun's heat. Rails sat on top of wooden sleepers and were held in place by iron supports. Sleepers sat on beds of crushed stones, called ballast.

People had to learn how to build strong, safe bridges and tunnels. Using dynamite to blow a hole in a mountain or drilling through rock is dangerous work. Falling rocks killed lots of railway workers. Railway bridges had to be strong enough to take heavy trains with loads of freight or passengers.

Trains meant that people could travel further than ever before to visit distant places and see exciting new sights. Depending on what they could afford to spend, people would buy first, second, or third class tickets:

- Wealthy first class passengers rode in the better front carriages with lots of windows, plenty of room for luggage and the most comfortable seats.
- Second class passengers were in simpler carriages in the middle of the train.
- Third class tickets were the cheapest of all – they meant riding at the back of the train with overcrowding, less comfort, and sometimes no seats, or even no roof!

Wagons loaded with freight and once pulled by horses, donkeys, or cattle, were towed by new, improved locomotives. By the 1840s, these freight trains carried all kinds of cargo long distances – things like building materials, coal, mail, and food all moved quickly and easily from place to place.

freight train

Each steam train needed a Locomotive Engineer to drive and control the train, and a Fireman to keep the fire going and making steam. Firemen had hard physical jobs – to shovel coal into the firebox and add water to the engine's boiler. They also made sure there was enough fuel on board before starting journeys, then they controlled the fire, raising or banking it when the train needed more or less power to pull up or go down hills. Firemen cleaned dust and soot from the engines, and took their orders from the Engineer.

On passenger trains, Conductors were responsible for keeping passengers safe, making sure they were in their right seats, and collecting their tickets.

About 80 years ago, diesel engines started to replace steam locomotives, as they were faster and cheaper to run. Diesel trains use oil to power a generator, which makes electricity to run motors that turn the wheels and move the train.

diesel train

The first electric trains were developed in Europe during the 1950s, and were much cleaner and faster than diesel or steam trains. Electric power comes to the trains from power lines above, or an extra rail that runs along beside the tracks.

Modern electric trains are quiet, fast and clean, making less pollution than either cars or planes. New electric railways are being built in cities around the world:

- some at street level for trains, trams or trolleys
- others underground
- some even up in the air, above the street for monorails.

Trains being designed nowadays are faster, more comfortable, and more reliable than ever before. Designers keep searching for ways to make improvements. Some have created new trains that don't have any wheels at all! They use powerful magnets to float above a special track. These new magnetic trains are called magnetic levitation trains, or maglevs.

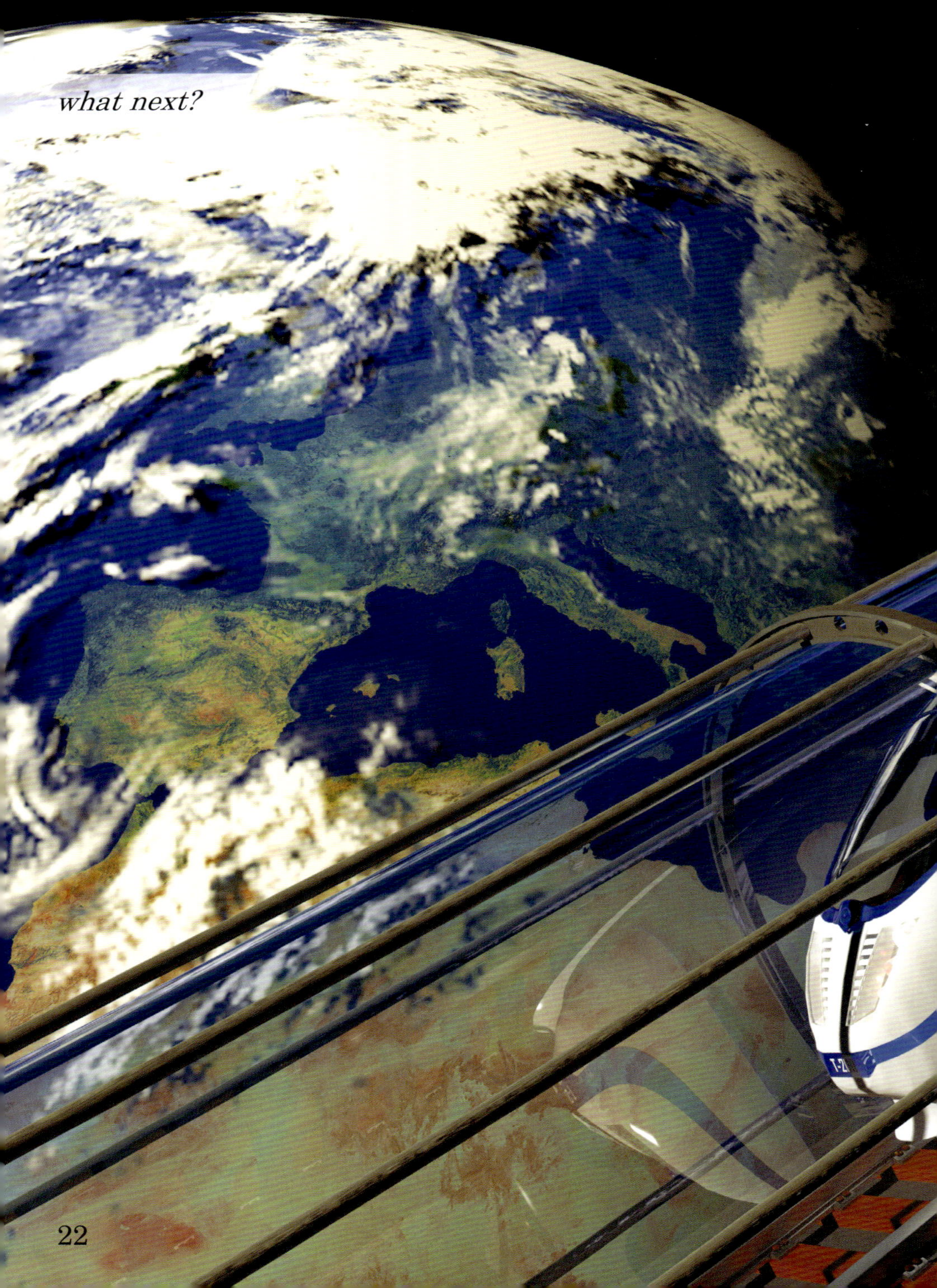
what next?

Trains have made a great difference in the world, and even changed the way people lived. Who knows how the trains of the future will transform our lives?
All aboard!